Puss in Boots

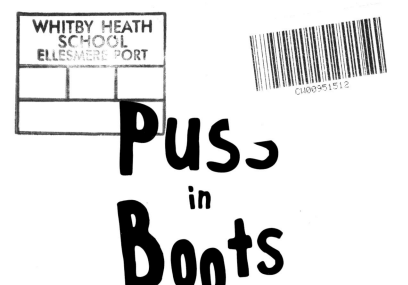

Original story by Charles Perrault

Retold by Pippa Goodhart

Series Advisor Professor Kimberley Reynolds

Illustrated by Thomas Radcliffe

OXFORD
UNIVERSITY PRESS

Letter from the Author

I grew up as one of three children, just like Jack in the story. I was the middle child, and it seemed to me that my brother and sister always got given things 'because he's the oldest' or 'because she's the youngest'. So, like Jack, I sometimes thought things were 'not fair'!

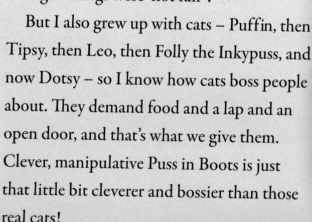

But I also grew up with cats – Puffin, then Tipsy, then Leo, then Folly the Inkypuss, and now Dotsy – so I know how cats boss people about. They demand food and a lap and an open door, and that's what we give them. Clever, manipulative Puss in Boots is just that little bit cleverer and bossier than those real cats!

Pippa Goodhart

An old miller died, leaving his mill to his eldest son. He left his donkey to his middle son, and the cat to his youngest son, Jack.

'We two older ones will work together,'
said the oldest son. 'We can make flour
at the mill. Then we can take the flour to
market on the donkey. We don't need a cat.
Goodbye, Jack!'

'That's not fair!' said Jack. 'What am I supposed to do with a cat? You will be rich and I will be poor. That's not fair at all!'

'Bad luck,' said his brothers.

But Jack didn't know that his cat wasn't an ordinary cat. His cat was the one and only Puss in Boots. Puss didn't just wear boots. He could talk. He said, 'No other cat is as clever as me. I *will* make you rich! Just wait and see!'

Puss took a basket. He went
to a field and he threw down grains
of corn. Then Puss hid. Rabbits came to
nibble the corn, and – *trap!* Puss caught
three rabbits.

Puss in Boots gave Jack one rabbit to cook for their supper.

'I might not be rich, but at least we will eat well tonight,' said Jack. 'Thank you, Puss.'

While Jack was busy chopping onions, Puss took the other two rabbits down the road to the King's palace.

Puss in Boots *knock knocked* at the palace door. It was opened by the King himself. Puss in Boots bowed very low.

'Your marvellous Majesty, here is a present from my master,' he said.

'Oh, how kind,' said the King. 'Tell me, who is your master?'

'My master is the Marquis of Carabas,' said Puss in Boots.

'Indeed?' said the King.
'Indeed,' said Puss in
Boots. He had made it all
up, but he looked at the
King and didn't blink, so
the King believed him.

'Then do please thank
the Marquis from me,' said
the King.

11

Puss in Boots purred as he and Jack ate their rabbit stew.

'This is all very nice,' said Jack. 'But I would still like to be rich, you know.'

'Ah, master, you must learn to trust me,' said Puss. 'I *will* still make you rich. Just wait and see.'

The next day, Puss in Boots set another
trap. This time he caught three partridges.

'Roast partridge for supper,' said Jack.
'And maybe some partridge feathers to
stuff my pillow? I may not be rich, but at
least I will be comfortable.'

While Jack was cooking supper, Puss in Boots walked down the road to the King's palace once again. *Knock knock.*

'Hello. I remember you, Puss,' said the King.

'Your marvellous Majesty,' said Puss in Boots, bowing low. 'Here is another present from the Marquis of Carabas.'

'Goodness, he *is* kind!' said the King, taking the partridges.

The day after that, Jack and Puss in Boots were walking along, when Puss said to Jack, 'Quick! Take off your clothes and get into the river.'

'What?' said Jack. 'Why should I?'

'You must just trust me. Do as I say. Then wait and see what happens,' said Puss.

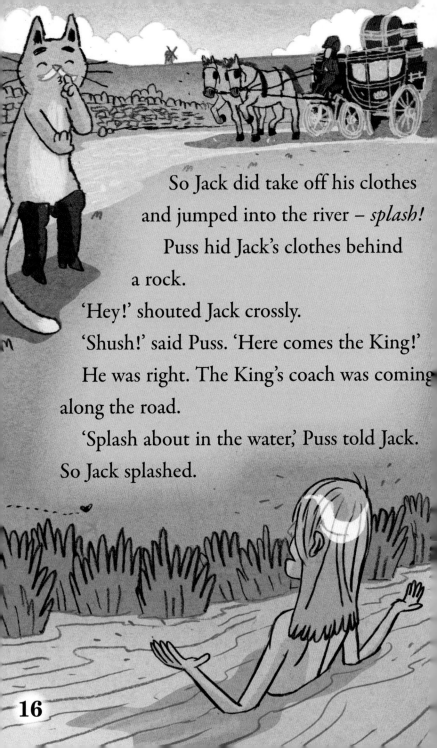

So Jack did take off his clothes
and jumped into the river – *splash!*
Puss hid Jack's clothes behind
a rock.

'Hey!' shouted Jack crossly.

'Shush!' said Puss. 'Here comes the King!'

He was right. The King's coach was coming
along the road.

'Splash about in the water,' Puss told Jack.
So Jack splashed.

Puss in Boots ran into the road. He waved his paws.

'Stop!' he shouted. 'Oh, please help me!' he said as the King put his head out of the window. 'My master, the Marquis of Carabas, was swimming in the river when somebody stole his clothes! Now he can't get out of the river because he has nothing to wear!'

'Goodness!' said the King. 'Stop the coach at once! The Marquis of Carabas has been so kind to me, I must help him. He can wear some of my clothes. Unpack them from my box!'

The King's footman handed fine clothes to Puss, and Puss handed them to Jack.

Jack quickly got dressed. Then he stepped forward.

'Thank you for the clothes,' he said. And Puss pushed him to make him bow down low.

'Not at all,' said the King. 'Not at all.'

Jack looked very handsome in the royal
clothes. The King's daughter noticed that.
The King told his daughter, 'Princess
Sophia, my dear, this young man is the
Marquis of Carabas. He has been so kind,
giving me presents. We must give him a lift
in our coach.'

'Yes, let's,' said Princess Sophia.

So the King and the Princess and Jack got into the coach, and they set off down the road.

Where was Puss in Boots? He ran ahead of the coach. Why? Because he had a clever plan. Wait and see!

There were people harvesting a fine crop of turnips in the fields. Puss ran over to them. He looked at the people fiercely, and he said, 'The King is coming! If he asks who owns all this land, tell him that it belongs to the Marquis of Carabas. If you don't, I'm going to be cross with you!' Puss showed them his claws.

Soon the King's coach came by. The King called from his coach window, 'Tell me, good people, whose fine land is this?' They all replied, 'It belongs to the Marquis of Carabas, Your Majesty.'

'Does it indeed!' said the King. *Goodness*, he thought. *This Marquis is a rich man.* And he gave Jack a smile.

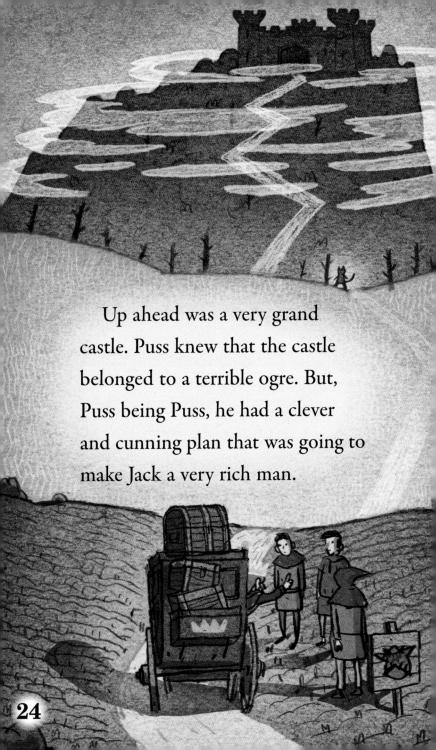

Up ahead was a very grand castle. Puss knew that the castle belonged to a terrible ogre. But, Puss being Puss, he had a clever and cunning plan that was going to make Jack a very rich man.

While the King was talking to the people in the field, Puss in Boots arrived at the castle door. *Knock knock.* The ogre opened the door.

'What do you want?' roared the ogre's big mouth full of terrible teeth.

'Oh marvellous Mr Ogre, sir,' said Puss, bowing low. 'I have heard such wonderful things about you! Now I have come to see for myself if what they say is true.'

'Wonderful things?' roared the ogre, pulling Puss inside. 'What wonderful things have you heard about me, pussy cat?'

'Well,' said Puss. 'I did hear that you can magic yourself into something even bigger than you already are.' Puss shook his head. 'But I didn't believe it.'

'Oh, but I can!' said the ogre. 'Watch this!' The ogre turned himself into a huge growly lion! Puss in Boots ran up the curtains to get away.

'That's all very well,' said Puss from up high. 'But turning into something big must be easy for a big ogre like you. I bet you can't make yourself really small.'

'Oh yes I can!' said the ogre. And he shrank into a tiny little mouse.

Down jumped Puss, and – *pounce!*
Puss in Boots ate that ogre mouse ...
just in time, because somebody was
knocking at the castle door.
Knock knock.

'Ah, Your marvellous Majesty!' said Puss
in Boots, opening the door and bowing
low. 'Welcome to the home of the Marquis
of Carabas!'

'Really?' said Jack.

'Absolutely!' said Puss in Boots.

'Goodness,' said the King.

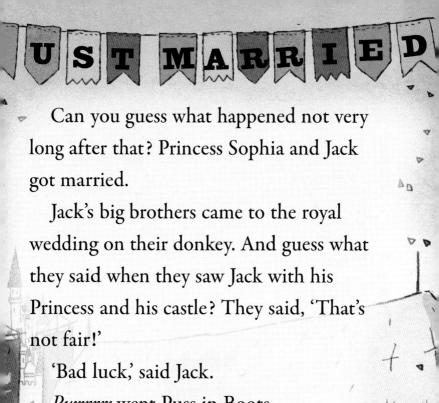

Can you guess what happened not very long after that? Princess Sophia and Jack got married.

Jack's big brothers came to the royal wedding on their donkey. And guess what they said when they saw Jack with his Princess and his castle? They said, 'That's not fair!'

'Bad luck,' said Jack.

Purrrrr went Puss in Boots.